Here's what kids and grown-ups have to say about the Magic Tree House® books:

"Oh, man . . . the Magic Tree House series
is really exciting!"
—Christina

"I like the Magic Tree House series. I stay up
all night reading them. Even on school nights!"
—Peter

"Jack and Annie have opened a door to a world
of literacy that I know will continue throughout
the lives of my students."
—Deborah H.

"As a librarian, I have seen many happy young
readers coming into the library to check out
the next Magic Tree House book in the series."
—Lynne H.

Magic Tree House® Merlin Missions

For a list of all the Magic Tree House® titles,
visit MagicTreeHouse.com.

MAGIC TREE HOUSE®
MERLIN MISSIONS

#6 SEASON OF THE SANDSTORMS

BY MARY POPE OSBORNE
ILLUSTRATED BY SAL MURDOCCA

A STEPPING STONE BOOK™

Random House 🏠 New York

To Paul Caringella,

a scholar in the House of Wisdom

Text copyright © 2005 by Mary Pope Osborne
Cover art and interior illustrations copyright © 2005 by Sal Murdocca

All rights reserved. Published in the United States by Random House Children's Books, a division of Penguin Random House LLC, New York. Originally published in hardcover as Magic Tree House #34 in 2005.

Random House and the colophon are registered trademarks and A Stepping Stone Book and the colophon are trademarks of Penguin Random House LLC.
Magic Tree House is a registered trademark of Mary Pope Osborne; used under license.

Visit us on the Web!
randomhousekids.com
MagicTreeHouse.com

Educators and librarians, for a variety of teaching tools, visit us at
RHTeachersLibrarians.com

The Library of Congress has cataloged the hardcover edition of this work as follows:
Osborne, Mary Pope.
Season of the sandstorms / by Mary Pope Osborne ; illustrated by Sal Murdocca. —
    p.   cm. — (Magic tree house ; #34)
"A Merlin mission." "A Stepping Stone book."
Summary: Guided by a magic rhyme, Jack and Annie travel to ancient Baghdad on a mission to help the caliph disseminate wisdom to the world.
ISBN 978-0-375-83031-0 (trade) — ISBN 978-0-375-93031-7 (lib. bdg.) —
ISBN 978-0-375-83032-7 (pbk.) — ISBN 978-0-375-89456-5 (ebook)
[1. Time travel—Fiction. 2. Magic—Fiction. 3. Brothers and sisters—Fiction.
4. Baghdad (Iraq)—History—Fiction. 5. Iraq—History—Fiction.] I. Murdocca, Sal, ill.
II. Title. III. Series: Osborne, Mary Pope.
Magic tree house series ; v #34.   PZ7.O81167Se   2005   [E]—dc22   2005000836

Printed in the United States of America
30 29 28 27 26 25 24 23 22

This book has been officially leveled by using the F&P Text Level Gradient™ Leveling System.

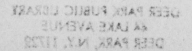

Dear Reader,

Many years ago, I journeyed overland from Greece to Nepal. On my trip, I traveled from Damascus, Syria, to Baghdad, Iraq, riding in a van through the desert. Just before sunset my traveling companion and I came upon a tea tent in the middle of nowhere. There, an old man and his great-grandson served tea to the few travelers who passed their way. The man and the boy invited us to share their dinner and camp near their tent. I'll never forget their kindness, nor the brilliant sunset over the desert—nor the cold starry night that followed. It has been a joy to return to these memories while writing Season of the Sandstorms, and I hope I can revisit the country of Iraq someday.

Mary Pope Osborne

CONTENTS

Away, for we are ready to a man!
Our camels sniff the evening and are glad.
Lead on, O Master of the Caravan:
Lead on the Merchant-Princes of Baghdad.
—James Elroy Flecker

Prologue

One summer day, a mysterious tree house appeared in the woods. A brother and sister named Jack and Annie soon learned that the tree house was magic—it could take them to any time and any place in history. They also learned that the tree house belonged to Morgan le Fay, a magical librarian from the legendary realm of Camelot.

After Jack and Annie traveled on many adventures for Morgan, Merlin the magician began sending them on "Merlin Missions" in the tree house. With help from two young sorcerers named Teddy and Kathleen, Jack and Annie visited four mythical places and found valuable objects to help save Camelot.

On their next four Merlin Missions, Jack and Annie were told they must travel to real times and real places in history and prove to Merlin that they could use magic wisely. They have just returned from a successful mission in the city of Venice over 250 years ago, and now they are waiting to hear from Merlin again. . . .

CHAPTER ONE

The Golden Age

Jack put his math homework aside. He opened the drawer beside his bed and pulled out a small, handmade book. For the hundredth time, he stared at the title on the cover:

10 MAGIC RHYMES FOR ANNIE AND JACK
FROM TEDDY AND KATHLEEN

For weeks, Jack had kept the book hidden in his drawer, wondering when he and Annie would be able to use its magic again. The book's ten rhymes were to be used on four missions, and each rhyme could be used only once. Jack and

Annie had already used two rhymes on a mission in Venice, Italy.

"Jack!" Annie rushed into Jack's room. Her eyes were shining. "Bring the book! Let's go!"

"Where?" said Jack.

"You know where! Come on!" Annie called as she ran back downstairs.

Jack quickly put Teddy and Kathleen's book into his backpack. He pulled on his jacket and took off down the stairs.

Annie was waiting on the front porch. "Hurry!" she cried.

"Wait! How do you know it's there?" Jack said.

"Because I just saw it!" Annie shouted. She hurried down the porch steps and crossed the yard.

"You saw it? Actually saw it?" yelled Jack as he followed Annie through the chilly afternoon air.

"Yes! Yes!" Annie yelled.

"When?" shouted Jack.

"Just now!" said Annie. "I was walking home from the library and I had this *feeling*—so I went and looked! It's waiting for us!"

Jack and Annie raced into the Frog Creek woods. They ran between the budding trees, over the fresh green moss of early spring, until they came to the tallest oak.

"See?" said Annie.

"Yes," breathed Jack. He stared up at the magic tree house. Its rope ladder dangled above the mossy ground. Annie started climbing up. Jack followed. When they got inside, Jack pulled off his backpack.

"Look, a book and a letter!" Annie said. She picked up a folded letter from the floor, and Jack picked up a book with a gold cover.

"Baghdad," Jack said. He showed the book to Annie. Its title was:

THE GOLDEN AGE OF BAGHDAD

"A golden age?" said Annie. "That sounds cool. Let's go!"

"Wait, we should read our letter first," said Jack.

"Right," said Annie. She unfolded the paper. "Merlin's handwriting," she said. She read aloud:

Dear Jack and Annie of Frog Creek,
Your mission is to journey to Baghdad of long
ago and help the caliph spread wisdom to
the world. To succeed, you must be humble
and use your magic wisely. Follow these—

"Wait, what's a *caliph?*" said Jack. "And what's Merlin mean—'spread wisdom to the world'? That's a big responsibility."

"I don't know," said Annie. "Let me finish." She kept reading:

Follow these instructions:
> *Ride a ship of the desert*
> *on a cold starry night.*
> *Ride through the dust*
> *and hot morning light.*

Find a horse on a dome,
the one who sees all,
in the heart of the city
behind the third wall.

Beneath birds who sing
in the Room of the Tree,
greet a friend you once knew
and a new friend to be.

Remember that life
is full of surprises.
Return to the tree house
before the moon rises.

—M.

"This sounds pretty easy," said Annie.

"No, it doesn't," said Jack. "All these instructions are so mysterious. We don't know what any of them mean."

"We'll find out when we get there," said Annie. "But first we have to get there. Make the wish."

"Okay," said Jack. He pointed to the cover of

the book. "I wish we could go to the golden age of Baghdad," he said.

The wind started to blow.

The tree house started to spin.

It spun faster and faster.

Then everything was still.

Absolutely still.

CHAPTER TWO

Nowhere

J ack felt hot. He opened his eyes. Burning sunlight was flooding into the tree house. He and Annie were wearing long robes tied with cords. They wore white head cloths and pointy slip-on shoes. Jack's backpack had turned into a leather shoulder bag.

"We look like characters in that book Aunt Mary gave us," said Annie, *"Tales from the Arabian Nights."*

"Yeah, like Aladdin and Ali Baba," said Jack.

Shading their eyes from the bright sunlight, Jack and Annie squinted out the window. They had landed in the spiky crown of a palm tree. It was the tallest tree in a clump of palm trees.

Thorny shrubs and sparse green grass grew under the trees. A small spring bubbled up from the ground. Surrounding the clump of trees were miles and miles of scorching sand.

"This doesn't look like a golden age to me," said Annie.

"Yeah, and where's Baghdad?" asked Jack. He picked up their research book and opened it to the first page. He read aloud:

> **From 762 AD to 1258 AD, the Arab world had a golden age. During that time, a ruler known as a caliph (say KAY-liff) governed an empire that stretched for thousands of miles. The capital of the Arab empire was the city of Baghdad, an important center for learning and trade.**

Jack looked up. "So the caliph is a ruler," he said, "and he probably lived in Baghdad."

"Yeah, but how do we *get* there?" asked Annie.

"Patience," said Jack. "Remember on our last

mission, we learned that we have to do things in order, one thing at a time." He read the first part of Merlin's instructions.

Ride a ship of the desert
on a cold starry night.
Ride through the dust
and hot morning light.

"I wonder what a 'ship of the desert' is," said Jack, looking up.

"Well, whatever it is, I'm sure we'll find it eventually," Annie said slowly, as if she were trying to sound patient. "We could just sit here and keep an eye out for a big boat. Or . . ."

"Or what?" said Jack.

"Maybe we could use one of Teddy and Kathleen's magic rhymes."

"Not yet," said Jack. "Merlin said to use our magic wisely. We just got here. We used two rhymes on our last mission. And we only have eight left to divide between three—"

"Okay, okay—" Annie broke in. "We can only

use a rhyme when there's absolutely nothing else to do, right?"

"Right," said Jack.

"So . . . ," said Annie. "What do *you* think we should do?"

"We could start walking," said Jack.

"Walk where?" said Annie. "Which way is Baghdad?"

Jack looked out the window. Beyond the palm trees there was nothing but sand and sky. In the distance were lonely dunes. The desert was eerily silent.

"We could, uh . . ." Jack couldn't think of anything else they could do. "We could look in the rhyme book," he said. Jack pulled the book of magic rhymes out of his pack. He and Annie read down the table of contents together.

"*Make a Stone Come Alive,*" read Annie. "We did that on our last mission. We can't do that again."

"It wouldn't help, anyway," said Jack. He looked at other rhymes. "*Make Metal Soft,*" he read. "We've already done that, too."

"*Turn into Ducks,*" read Annie. She looked at Jack.

"No," he said.

"*Mend What Cannot Be Mended,*" read Annie.

"Nothing needs mending," said Jack.

"How about *this* one?" said Annie. "*Make Helpers Appear out of Nowhere.*"

"Well . . . ," said Jack. "Maybe . . ."

"Come on, it's perfect," said Annie. "That's where we are—nowhere. And we could sure use some helpers."

"Okay," said Jack. "I'll read the line Teddy wrote. You read Kathleen's line in her selkie language."

"Okay," said Annie. She turned to the page with the rhyme. She held the book out to Jack.

Jack read in a loud, clear voice:

From far beyond, send helpers here!

Then Annie read:

Hah-ee-by, hah-ee-keer!

The second that Annie finished the rhyme,

wind gusted in from the desert, blowing a cloud of sand through the window. The wind shook the palm trees. Sand blew into Annie's eyes. "Oww!" she said.

"Get back!" cried Jack.

Jack and Annie jumped away from the window. They pressed themselves against the wall and covered their faces. Gritty sand kept blowing into the tree house.

"It's a sandstorm!" said Jack.

The hot sand piled into drifts all over the floor. Then the wind died down as quickly as it had started. The palm trees stopped shaking.

Jack and Annie looked out the window. The air was thick with grainy dust, making it hard to see. But the sand was still.

"I think it's over," said Annie.

"I hope so," said Jack. "Why did our magic rhyme cause a sandstorm instead of sending us helpers?"

"I don't know," said Annie. "Maybe we said it wrong."

Jack brushed the sand off their research book and looked up *sandstorms* in the index. He found the right page and read:

> **The season of the sandstorms begins in the desert in mid-February and continues all spring. Winds can blow as fast as 40 miles per hour. Sandstorms can easily cause travelers to lose their way in the desert.**

"I don't understand," said Jack. "We don't need to lose our way. We need to *find* our way."

Just then the sound of bells came from outside.

Jack and Annie looked out the window. Through the haze, they saw four riders perched high on the humps of camels. The riders wore brightly colored robes. Behind them a dozen more camels were tied head to tail and loaded down with saddlebags. As the camels swung from side to side, bells tinkled from around their necks.

Annie grinned. "Helpers!" she said.

CHAPTER THREE

Mamoon

Annie stuck her head out the tree house window. "Hey!" she called.

"Shhhh!" said Jack, pulling her back in. "Don't let them see us up here! It's too hard to explain the tree house. Let's go down."

"Good point," said Annie. She handed Merlin's letter to Jack and started down the rope ladder. Jack grabbed his shoulder bag. He put the letter inside, then added their research book and rhyme book. He slung the leather bag across his chest and climbed down.

When he stepped onto the ground, Jack twisted the rope ladder behind the tree trunk so it wouldn't be noticed. "Okay," he said to Annie.

"Hey!" Annie called again, waving. She and Jack stepped out into the open.

The camel riders headed toward the palm trees. The man in the lead made his camel kneel. As he climbed off, Jack and Annie ran over to him. The man wore a long white robe. He had a black beard and stern, dark eyes. "Who are you?" he asked, unsmiling. "From where do you come?"

"I am Annie, and this is my brother, Jack," said Annie. "Our home is far away in Frog Creek, Pennsylvania."

"I have not heard of such a place," the man said. "How do you come to be here in the desert alone?"

"Uh . . ." Jack didn't know what to say.

"We were riding with our family," Annie said. "We stopped to rest here. My brother and I took a nap behind these trees. When we woke up, everyone was gone. They left us by mistake. See, we have a really *big* family. There are many brothers and sisters—"

"Annie," said Jack. She was saying too much, he thought.

The man looked concerned. "Why have they not come back for you?" he said, gazing out at the desert. "I hope they have not been attacked by bandits."

"Are there bandits around here?" asked Annie.

"There are many bandits prowling the desert," said the man.

Jack looked anxiously around at the vast sandy plain.

"That is why one must always travel with others," said the man. "But I hope your family is safe and will return for you soon."

"Excuse me," Annie said politely. "But who are you? How did you happen to come here?"

"I am a merchant," the man said. "My caravan was traveling from the west, when we were surprised by a sudden sandstorm. It seemed to come from nowhere. But luckily it brought us to this oasis. We will rest and water our animals until the sun goes down. In the cool of the night, we will travel on to Baghdad."

The caravan leader walked over to his men and spoke to them. They dismounted and started taking saddlebags off the camels.

Annie turned to Jack. "See, our rhyme worked!" she whispered. "The sandstorm was magic! It brought them here on their way to Baghdad!"

"But how can we get *them* to help us?" said Jack.

"Well, Merlin said we should be humble, so let's offer to help *them*," said Annie. She walked over to the caravan leader. He was filling a canvas bucket with water from a small spring.

"Excuse me," said Annie, "we wondered if we could help you."

The man gave her a quick smile. "Thank you, yes," he said. "If you could gather dates, it would be most appreciated. My men are very hungry." He handed Annie two large baskets.

"No problem," said Annie. "We'll gather dates."

Annie carried the baskets to Jack. "Do you know what a *date* is?" she whispered. "We're supposed to gather some."

"I'll look it up," said Jack. With his back to the

camel riders, he pulled their research book out of his bag and looked up *dates*. He read:

> **Dates are known as the fruit of the desert. They hang in bunches from date palms. People gather dates by shaking the trunk of the tree. Not only are dates an important food, but the wood and leaves of the date palm are used to make—**

"Okay, got it," interrupted Annie, putting the baskets down. "Let's start shaking the trees!"

Jack put the book away and looked around. For the first time, he noticed bunches of brown fruit hanging from the trees. He grabbed hold of the nearest tree trunk. Annie grabbed the trunk from the other side. Together they shook the tree until dates began falling to the ground.

In the desert heat, Jack and Annie went from tree to tree, shaking each one and gathering the dates that fell to the ground. By the time they had filled their baskets, the trees were casting long shadows over the oasis.

Tired and sweaty, Jack and Annie carried their heavy baskets back to the caravan leader. He was boiling water over a fire of twigs. "Ah, very good," he said. "Thank you, Jack and Annie."

"You're welcome," said Annie. "What else can we do for you?"

"You should rest from the heat now," said the man. "Would you like to sit and have tea with us?"

"Sure," said Annie. "By the way, what's your name?"

"My name is very long," the man said with a smile. "You may call me Mamoon."

While their camels grazed, Mamoon and his men sat on a woolen rug spread over the grass. They shared dates and tea with Jack and Annie. The dark, plump fruit was sweet and chewy. The tea was strong but good.

In the fiery red glow of the setting sun, Jack watched the grazing camels. He thought the humped animals looked really funny. They had knobby knees, big clumsy feet, and little ears that twitched. Some camels smacked their droopy lips as they drank water. Others gobbled down whole branches of thornbushes without chewing.

"Don't the thorns hurt the camels' throats?" Jack asked Mamoon.

"No," said the caravan leader. "Their mouths are very tough. They can eat anything: sticks, bones—"

"Even our tents and saddlebags if we let them!" said a young camel rider.

Annie and Jack laughed. "What's in your saddlebags?" Annie asked.

"Our bags are filled with goods from Greece, Turkey, and Syria," said Mamoon. "We have many things: jewels, beads, and precious spices, such as cinnamon, pepper, and vanilla. We are taking everything to Baghdad to sell."

"We have to get to Baghdad, too," said Annie.

"We have to meet with the caliph."

The camel riders chuckled as if they thought Annie was making a joke.

Only Mamoon did not laugh. "Your family is to meet with the caliph?" he said.

"No," said Annie. "Just Jack and me. We have to help him spread wisdom to the world."

"*Annie,*" warned Jack.

The camel riders laughed loudly.

"What's so funny?" Annie asked.

"The caliph does not meet with children," said a young man. "He is the most powerful and important person in the world."

"Oh," said Annie, frowning.

The news worried Jack, too.

Mamoon looked at Annie and Jack with a curious expression. "Night will soon be upon us. Since your family has not yet returned, would you like to travel with us to Baghdad?" he said. "You have journeyed by camel this far. I trust you can ride camels the rest of the way."

"Sure we can!" said Annie. "We *love* camels!"

We do? thought Jack.

"Good. We love our ships of the desert, too," said Mamoon. "We will set sail on them soon."

"So that's what 'ships of the desert' are!" Annie whispered to Jack.

Camels, thought Jack. *Oh, brother*.

CHAPTER FOUR

Ships of the Desert

The camel riders all silently watched the sun set over the faraway dunes. As the fiery ball slipped beneath the horizon, the desert was flooded with red light. As soon as the sun disappeared, the air grew much cooler.

Mamoon stood up. "It is time to go," he said.

The camel riders put out their small fire. In the growing darkness, Mamoon helped them saddle up their animals and load them with baggage.

Then Mamoon came over to Jack and Annie. "You can ride those two sisters," he said, pointing to two camels kneeling in the sand. "Climb on, then come to the front of the line to ride with me."

Jack and Annie walked over to the two camel sisters. Each had reins hanging from her neck. Saddles made from colorful cushions were piled high on their humps.

Annie patted the wiry, tan-colored fur of one of the camels. The camel looked at Annie with big eyes and fluttered her thick eyelashes. "Hey, Cutie," said Annie.

The other camel nuzzled Annie's neck. "Hey, Beauty," Annie said to the other. "You want some attention, too?"

"*Cutie* and *Beauty*?" said Jack. He didn't find either camel particularly cute *or* beautiful.

Annie climbed onto Cutie's saddle cushion and picked up the reins. "Let's ride!" she said.

Cutie rose awkwardly up from a kneeling position to a full stand. "Oh, wow!" said Annie, towering over Jack. "She's really tall."

Jack started to climb onto Beauty. But the

camel caught an end of his head cloth and began chewing it.

"Stop that!" said Jack, pulling the cloth away from her. Beauty opened her mouth wide and flashed rows of sharp teeth. Jack drew back.

"Don't be afraid," said Annie.

"Easy for *you* to say," said Jack. "Yours likes you."

"Don't worry, Beauty likes you, too," said Annie. "I can tell." Annie's camel began ambling toward the other camels waiting to head off into the desert. "Come on, Jack! It's really fun once you're moving!" she called.

"Fun," muttered Jack. "Right." He held on to the ends of his head cloth and put his leg over Beauty's hump. The camel eyed him suspiciously. She swished her tail, slapping his back.

"Hey!" said Jack.

Jack tried to get comfortable on the saddle cushion. But Beauty spat at him and made a weird screeching sound.

"Quiet!" said Jack. He hooked his shoulder bag onto a saddle horn. When he was finally settled, Beauty turned her head and started chewing on his leather bag.

"No! Don't!" yelled Jack. He tried pulling the bag away, but Beauty played tug-of-war. "Come on, let go," Jack said. "Give it back, stupid!"

"Do you really think she is stupid?"

Jack jumped. Mamoon had ridden up behind him and was watching as he tried to get his bag back from Beauty.

Jack was embarrassed. "Um, she won't let go of my stuff," he said.

Mamoon grabbed the strap of Jack's bag. He clucked his tongue, and the camel let go. She groaned as Mamoon hooked the leather bag back onto the saddle horn.

"For thousands of years, camels like this one have carried people across the desert," said Mamoon. "She is truly a miracle of nature."

Some miracle, thought Jack.

"She can drink two barrels of water in ten minutes," said Mamoon, "and then go for a week without drinking again. She can live many days without food, too."

"Really?" said Jack.

"She is well suited to travel in the desert," said Mamoon. "Her thick eyebrows protect her eyes from the glare of the sun. Her long eyelashes and the fur around her ears keep out the windblown sand."

"Cool," said Jack softly.

"Her feet are so tough, they do not feel the heat of the desert," said Mamoon. "And they are so big that they keep her from sinking down into the loose sand."

"Hmm," said Jack.

"She can carry five hundred pounds of baggage on her back," said Mamoon, "and travel one hundred miles in a single day."

"That's a lot," murmured Jack.

Mamoon tugged on the camel's reins and

clucked his tongue. Beauty breathed heavily as she rose up on her long, powerful legs to her full height.

Mamoon looked at Jack. "We must respect her and honor her," he said. "In many ways, she is superior to us, no?"

Jack nodded. He thought of the words of Merlin's letter. *To succeed in your mission, you must be humble.* He patted the camel. "Good girl, Beauty."

Mamoon clucked his tongue again to coax the camel forward. Perched high on his saddle, Jack rocked from side to side. He did not feel at all safe, but he stayed calm. Beauty ambled over to Cutie. The two sisters stood together and snorted.

The desert sky was bright with stars. Mamoon called to his men, and the caravan started moving forward.

The camels walked with a swaying motion. They moved two big feet on one side, then two

big feet on the other. Jack gripped the horn of his saddle as his "ship of the desert" rocked from left to right.

"Isn't this fun?" said Annie, rocking alongside him.

"Sort of," said Jack, shivering. Actually, he wasn't having any fun at all. He felt seasick and was freezing in the night air. Also, he was worried about their mission. Would the caliph meet with them? If he did, how could they help him "spread wisdom to the world"? And if Baghdad was very far away, how would they ever find their way back to the tree house?

Mamoon slowed his camel until he was riding between Jack and Annie. "When I was a boy, I spent many cold nights in the desert riding with my father on journeys to the west," he said. "At first, I, too, thought camels were foolish. I always longed for more blankets and for a smoother ride. I wished to be back in Baghdad in my own warm bed."

Jack smiled. He liked the caravan leader.

"But over time, I have come to love the cold desert nights," said Mamoon. "Now when I am sleeping in my warm bed in Baghdad, I long to be here instead. I wish to be reading the wind and the stars."

"How do you read the stars?" asked Annie.

"They have their own language," said Mamoon. "At this moment, we are heading east, toward the Goat Star." He pointed at the sky.

Jack couldn't tell which star was the Goat Star. But he was filled with wonder. Thousands of tiny lights twinkled in the black dome of night. There were more stars than Jack had ever imagined. Some looked close enough to touch.

Mamoon started singing a song. The other camel riders joined in. Jack couldn't understand the words, but the tune was soothing. The camels seemed to sway to the music.

Jack stopped worrying about how they would get back to the tree house. And he found he was actually enjoying the fresh desert air. He started to relax.

"Jack," Annie said softly. "Guess what—we

just solved the first mystery in Merlin's letter: *Ride a ship of the desert on a cold starry night.*"

"Yeah," said Jack happily. "And it's really fun."

Suddenly a fierce shout came from the distance. Jack sat up straighter. His heart thumped.

"Bandits!" one of the camel drivers shouted.

CHAPTER FIVE

Bandits!

Jack looked around wildly. Dark figures on horses were galloping across the sand toward them. They were yelling and shouting.

"Oh, no!" cried Jack. "What should we do?"

"We will fight them off!" said Mamoon. "You and Annie take this box and ride to the dunes!" Mamoon pulled a flat wooden box out of one of his saddlebags. He thrust the box into Jack's hands. "Hurry! Ride as fast as you can! Protect it with your lives!"

Jack frantically tried to stuff the box into

his shoulder bag. But Mamoon slapped the back of Jack's camel, and she bolted forward. The reins slipped from Jack's hands. He grabbed the saddle horn with one hand and clutched the wooden box to his chest with the other. He held on for his life as Beauty galloped across the dark desert.

Annie's camel ran beside Jack's. Like two racehorses, Beauty and Cutie thundered across the sand toward the distant dunes. Rocking crazily from side to side, Jack clung to the box. "Slow down!" he yelled. "Please!"

It was no use. Beauty ran like the wind. She and her sister practically flew over the desert under the starry sky. Jack wanted the camels to stop. But at the same time, he wanted to get far away from the bandits.

Finally the camels began to slow their pace. Jack looked back. He couldn't see the caravan at all, and no one seemed to be following them.

When the two camels reached the dunes, they began plodding around the steep hills. Once they were nestled safely between tall sand drifts, they stopped to rest. Beauty grunted. Cutie snorted.

"Thanks . . . thanks, girls," said Annie, panting.

"I hope Mamoon and the others are safe from the bandits," said Jack.

"Me too," said Annie. "What's in the box he gave us?"

Jack held up the flat wooden box. "I don't know," he said. "But Mamoon said we should protect it with our lives."

"Maybe it's a precious spice," said Annie.

"I hope it's more than *that*," said Jack. "I'd hate to risk my life for cinnamon or pepper."

"Should we look?" said Annie.

"I don't know," said Jack. "Mamoon might not want us to."

"But don't you think we could protect it better if we knew what it was?" said Annie.

"Maybe . . . ," said Jack. He could see Annie's point. "Okay."

Jack tried to open the lid of the box, but he couldn't. In the dark, his finger pressed against a keyhole. "Forget it," he said. "It's locked."

"Shh! Listen!" said Annie.

Jack listened. He heard a high-pitched moaning sound. It sounded like music from a violin. Wafting through the dry sand dunes, the haunting music grew louder.

"What *is* that?" said Jack.

"Uh-oh," said Annie. "Now I hear something else."

Jack held his breath. He heard hooves galloping over the desert. "The bandits!" he said.

"We have to hide the box!" said Annie.

"Where?" said Jack.

"In the sand!" said Annie. She clucked her tongue, and Cutie knelt down to the ground. Beauty knelt, too. Jack and Annie jumped off their saddle cushions and started digging in the sand.

The sound of hoofbeats grew louder and louder. Jack and Annie dug frantically. They threw sand behind them like puppies digging in the dirt.

"That's deep enough!" said Jack. He placed the box in the hole they had dug. Then he and Annie pushed piles of sand back on top of it.

When they stood up, Annie gasped. "Look!"

A dark figure on a camel was silhouetted against the starlit sky. The rider was winding his way through the dunes toward them. Jack's heart nearly pounded out of his chest.

"Should we use a magic rhyme?" Annie asked.

"We don't have time!" said Jack.

The rider drew closer, until he stopped in front of Jack and Annie. "You are safe, no?" he said.

"Mamoon!" said Annie.

Relief flooded through Jack. He laughed. "Yes, we're safe!" he said. "And *you're* safe, too!"

"My men fought well," said Mamoon. "The

thieves fled with only a few bags of pepper and painted beads."

"And we kept your box safe, too!" said Annie proudly. She knelt and dug in the sand until she uncovered the wooden box. She handed it to Mamoon.

"Ahh, very good," the caravan leader said.

"What's in the box?" asked Annie.

"A priceless treasure," said Mamoon. "I have brought it all the way from Greece. And I am taking it to Baghdad. Thank you both for guarding it with your lives. You are very special."

"Sure, no problem," said Jack. He still wondered what was in the box. *Gold? Silver? Precious jewels?*

But Mamoon did not say. He put the box back into his camel's saddlebag. "Let us be on our way now," he said.

Jack climbed on top of his kneeling camel. He clucked his tongue. He was surprised and pleased when Beauty rose up on her tall legs.

"We will catch up with the others in Baghdad," said Mamoon. "If all goes well, we will arrive in the city in the afternoon. We must head east toward the morning sun."

Mamoon rode out of the dunes. Jack and Annie followed him. As their camels rocked through the chilly dawn, daylight shimmered over the sand.

"Mamoon, last night we heard strange sounds in the dunes," said Annie. "Like music playing."

"Ah, yes," said Mamoon, "*the whistling sands.*"

"What are the whistling sands?" asked Jack.

"Some say it is magic," said Mamoon. "But I believe that all things in nature have their reasons. That is why I like the study of *science*. Science says we must observe our world. We must make experiments and try to find out why things happen. We have learned the whistling is made by sands settling in the drifts."

"Oh," said Annie. "I'd hoped it was magic."

"Learning the reasons for things *is* magic,"

said Mamoon. "True knowledge brings light to the world. And that is a magical thing, no?"

"Yes," said Jack.

Annie nodded thoughtfully. "I guess, when you put it that way," she said.

Swaying from side to side on their camels, the three riders traveled toward the dawn. As the sun rose higher in the sky, the desert grew blazing hot. A dry wind whipped through the air, making snaky patterns in the sand.

Mamoon halted his camel. He looked around and frowned.

"What's wrong?" said Jack. "Are there signs of bandits?"

Mamoon shook his head. "No, it is the desert itself that worries me now," he said. "It is restless." He clucked his tongue, and his camel began walking again.

As they rode over the restless desert, the wind picked up loose sand and tossed it into the air. Jack and Annie lowered their heads to keep the sand from blowing into their eyes. Their head cloths flapped in the wind. More and more sand started blowing. The desert seemed alive as the sand shifted and swirled.

Mamoon stopped again and looked about. The snaky patterns in the sand were blowing into round, curly patterns. Jack heard a weird moaning sound. "Is that the whistling sands again?" he asked hopefully.

"No," said Mamoon. "That is the cry of a terrible sandstorm. And it will soon be upon us."

CHAPTER SIX

Sandblasted

In the distance, a haze of sand was spreading over the desert. As the wind picked up, the sky turned red and the haze thickened into a brown cloud. The cloud began gliding toward Jack, Annie, and Mamoon like a moving wall.

"Get down! Lie on your bellies!" ordered Mamoon. "Quickly! Cover your faces with your head cloths!"

Jack clucked his tongue. Beauty knelt to the ground. Jack, Annie, and Mamoon jumped off their camels and lay down on the sand beside them.

Jack tried desperately to cover his face with his head cloth, but the raging wind kept whipping the cloth from his hands. The sky turned from red to black. The moaning sound turned into a loud rumbling.

Jack looked up and saw the wind rip the saddlebag off Mamoon's kneeling camel! The bag hit the ground and fell open. The box bounced out and tumbled away in the driving wind.

"The treasure!" cried Jack, but his voice was drowned out by the wind. He jumped up and bolted after the box.

Jack raced across the desert as the sand battered his body. The wind tried to push him down. But Jack ran with all his might, until finally he caught up with the box and threw himself down on top of it. He grabbed the ends of his head scarf and covered his face.

The sandstorm blasted over Jack, sounding like the hoofbeats of a hundred galloping camels. Jack's eyes burned. He felt as if he were suffocating.

Slowly the thundering softened to a low rumbling. The rumbling faded to a moaning. The wind died down. The hot desert grew still and silent.

Coughing, Jack rolled over and sat up. He had sand in his mouth, sand in his ears, and sand in his nose. He pulled off his glasses and rubbed his stinging eyes. But rubbing only made them worse.

Blinking, Jack clutched the box and looked around for the others. The air was thick with dust. He had completely lost his sense of direction.

"Jack! Jack!" He heard Annie shouting.

Jack clutched the small wooden box and stood up. His legs were so wobbly, he fell over. "Annie!" he croaked.

"Jack!" she called through the dust. "Where are you?"

"Here!" he said.

"Where?"

"Here!"

"*There* you are!" said Annie, stumbling out of the haze. "Are you okay?"

"I'm okay," croaked Jack. "Are you?"

"Yes! I ran after you," said Annie. Her voice was hoarse, too.

"I had to save the box," said Jack. "Where's Mamoon?"

"I don't know," said Annie. "I don't think he saw us chase after the box."

"Mamoon!" they shouted together. "Mamoon!"

There was no answer.

Peering through the sandy haze, Jack heard thumping sounds. He and Annie turned around. Their two camels were trotting toward them.

"Cutie!" cried Annie. "Beauty!"

Jack and Annie stumbled to their camels and grabbed their reins.

"Thank you for finding us!" said Annie.

"Yeah, thanks," said Jack, patting Beauty.

"Mamoon!" Annie called. "Mamoon!"

"He must have gone in the wrong direction to look for us," said Jack.

"If we don't find him, how will we get to Baghdad? And what will we do with his treasure?" asked Annie.

"I don't know," said Jack. He held up the wooden box.

"Look, the top's broken," said Annie. She pointed to a long crack running down the lid of the box.

"I hope the treasure wasn't hurt," said Jack.

"Maybe we should check and see," said Annie.

Jack took a deep breath. He still thought Mamoon might not want them to look inside the box. But his curiosity got the best of him. "Okay," he said. "I guess it wouldn't hurt to make sure it's all right."

Jack pried apart the two pieces of wood and lifted them off. Inside the box was a book.

"A book?" said Jack, surprised. He'd expected gold or jewels. He carefully lifted the book out of the box. It had a plain leather cover with no title on it.

"It doesn't *look* like a precious treasure," said Annie.

"Maybe the writing inside is the treasure," said Jack.

Jack gently opened the book. Inside were pages of thick yellow paper. The pages were bound with stitching and covered with writing on both sides. The first page said:

THE WRITINGS OF ARISTOTLE

"Who is Ar-is-totle?" said Annie, sounding out the name.

"I don't know," said Jack. "I'll look him up in our research book." He unhooked his bag from the saddle horn. Sand covered the books inside. He pulled out their research book and brushed it off. Then he looked up *Aristotle* in the index. "Good. He's here," Jack said. He turned to the right page and read:

> **Aristotle (say AIR-is-TAH-tul) lived in ancient Greece over 2,300 years ago. He is known as one of the greatest philosophers of all time. The word *philosopher* means "lover of wisdom." Aristotle's works were introduced to the Western world by the Arabs in the Middle Ages.**

"So Aristotle was a great lover of wisdom," said Annie.

"I guess so," said Jack. "But I wonder why this book is such a treasure."

"Wait a minute," said Annie. "Doesn't Merlin's

note tell us that we have to help the caliph of Baghdad spread *wisdom* to the world?"

Jack caught his breath. "Yeah," he said. "And if this is a book of Aristotle's writings, it must be full of wisdom.... We have to get this book to the caliph—that's our mission for Merlin!"

"We better get going!" said Annie.

Jack and Annie pulled on the reins of their camels and clucked their tongues. Beauty and Cutie knelt in the sand, and Jack and Annie climbed on. Leaving the broken box behind, Jack carefully packed the ancient book of Aristotle's wisdom and the research book into his bag. Then he hung the bag from his saddle horn.

"Which way?" said Annie.

"Toward the rising sun in the east," said Jack. "That's what Mamoon said."

"It's that way, then," said Annie. She pointed toward a bright blur in the hazy sky.

Jack and Annie's camels headed into the dusty, glaring sun. "Hey, we're following Merlin's second instruction now," said Annie. *"Ride through the dust and hot morning light."*

"You're right," said Jack.

As Jack and Annie kept traveling toward the east, the desert sands shimmered and sparkled with heat. The air cleared, but still they saw no sign of Mamoon.

Jack looked down to shield his eyes from the burning sunlight. Exhausted, he closed his eyes. As Beauty swayed gently from side to side, Jack's head dropped forward. Suddenly he heard Annie shout, "Jack! Look!"

"What? Mamoon?" said Jack, jerking awake.

"No! Look!" said Annie.

In the distance, Jack saw sunlit towers and domes shining against the clear blue sky. "Oh, man," he whispered. *"Baghdad."*

CHAPTER SEVEN

Behind the Third Wall

"Let's hurry!" said Annie.

As Beauty and Cutie walked toward Baghdad, the loose sand of the desert changed to sunbaked earth. Then the hard earth changed to scrubby grass. Goats and sheep grazed in the grass, and farms dotted the countryside.

It wasn't long before Jack and Annie came to a red clay path. The path led to a crossroads where many travelers were coming from different directions. They were all heading toward the shining city. Jack and Annie rode alongside boys driving sheep and farmers in donkey carts. They passed women with veils over their faces, carrying pots on their shoulders.

Jack kept looking for Mamoon. But he never saw him. Moving with the crowd, Beauty and

Cutie clomped across a bridge. Rowboats and barges glided along the yellowish brown river.

On the other side of the river was a huge outdoor market with a maze of tents. The market seemed to be filled with people from many countries. The sharp smell of incense filled the air. Stalls were jammed with burlap sacks, baskets, and carpets. Shoemakers sat cross-legged, stitching shoes. Potters were bent over ovens, baking earth-colored pots. Weavers sat at small looms, spinning silk brocade.

"Paper? Pearls?" a merchant shouted.

"No thanks!" said Annie.

"Pigeons, parrots?" another shouted at Jack.

"No thanks!" he said.

"I love this place!" said Annie. "What is it?"

"I'll look it up," said Jack. He pulled out their research book and read:

> In the ninth century, traders from all over the world brought their goods to Baghdad to sell. Baghdad merchants

traded paper, fine cloth, and jewelry for goods from Spain, India, Africa, China, Greece, and other lands. These goods were sold in a huge open-air market called a bazaar.

"Oh, so a *bazaar* is sort of like a mall," said Jack.

"It's a lot *better* than a mall!" said Annie. "Let's get off and look around."

"We don't have time to shop," said Jack. "We have to finish our mission." He pulled out Merlin's letter and read:

Find a horse on a dome,
the one who sees all,
in the heart of the city
behind the third wall.

"It sounds like we pass three walls and then we come to a horse," said Jack. "We'd better keep going."

Jack put the book and letter away. Beauty and Cutie ambled through the noisy bazaar.

When they left the bazaar, they came to a curved brick wall. Running along the base of the wall was a muddy moat.

"Look—that must be the first wall!" said Annie.

"Cool," said Jack.

Jack and Annie rode the two camels over an arched bridge that crossed the moat. They passed through a gate with double iron doors. On the other side of the wall was a busy avenue lined with buildings.

As their camels wove slowly in and out of the crowd, Jack pulled out their research book. Swaying from side to side, he read to Annie:

> **During its golden age, Baghdad had good hospitals. The city was also known for its excellent police system and public schools, along with its many libraries and stores and a zoo with a hundred lions.**

"I'd like to visit those lions," said Annie.

"We don't have time now," said Jack.

Their camels clopped down the busy avenue until they came to a green field.

"Look, there's the second wall!" said Annie.

Bordering the field was another wall. It was curved, too, but much taller than the first. It looked like it was at least a hundred feet high. There were guards at the gate, but they didn't seem to be checking any of the people passing through.

"Act normal," Jack advised Annie. "Don't attract their attention."

Jack and Annie joined a stream of people passing through the gate. Beyond the second wall was another grand avenue. And at the end of the wide cobbled road was another green field. "Look! The third wall!" said Annie.

The third wall was even taller than the second. Again, people were passing freely through its gate.

"This part of the mission is easy!" said Annie.

"Yeah," said Jack. "But we still have to find that horse on the dome, and then find the caliph and get him to meet with us."

Beauty and Cutie ambled through the gate of the third wall, carrying Jack and Annie into the heart of Baghdad. A palace loomed before them. Its roof was a glittering green dome. At the top of the dome stood the statue of a horse.

"Yay, the horse who sees all!" said Annie. "I'll bet the caliph lives in that palace. Let's follow those people inside." She pointed to a stream of people entering an arched passageway outside the palace.

Jack and Annie rode under the arch and into a beautiful garden. The warm breeze smelled of flowers. They rode down a path bordered by date palms until they came to a courtyard where boys were playing ball. Near the courtyard was a stable with camels in it.

"Looks like we'll have to go the rest of the way on foot," said Jack.

"Yeah, I guess Beauty and Cutie can stay there," said Annie, pointing to the stable.

Jack and Annie rode into the stable. They clucked, and the camels knelt. As Jack reached for his shoulder bag, a ball rolled into the stable. Annie picked it up and stepped outside. Jack followed her.

"Here!" shouted a young boy with curly black hair. He was holding out his hands. Annie threw the ball to him, and the boy caught it. He grinned at Annie's good throw. "Who are you?" he called. "Where are you from?"

Before Jack could say anything, Annie crossed to the boys. Jack hurried after her.

"I'm Annie and this is my brother, Jack," Annie said. "We're from Frog Creek, Pennsylvania."

"Why have you come to Baghdad?" the boy asked.

"We have to see the caliph," said Annie.

The boy and his friends laughed.

"What's so funny?" said Annie.

"Our caliph is the most powerful man in the world," said another boy. "He does not have time to visit with children."

"That's what everyone keeps saying," said Annie. "But we're here on a very important mission. We—"

"Annie," Jack interrupted, "come on. I left my bag back in the stable." He waved to the boys. "See you guys later. Let's go, Annie."

Annie started to leave with Jack.

"When you discover that the caliph will not meet with you, come back and play with us," called the curly-haired boy.

Annie stopped. "Don't worry," she called back. "He'll meet with us! We're special!"

"Annie, come on," said Jack.

"Why are *you* special?" shouted the boy.

"For one thing, we just saved a precious treasure from bandits and from a sandstorm in the desert," said Annie. "For another—"

"Annie!" Jack said sternly. He grabbed her arm. "Come *on*!" He pulled Annie away.

As they headed back into the stable, Jack shook his head. "Don't say stuff like that," he said.

"Why not?" said Annie.

"Because it's bragging," said Jack. "It makes other kids feel bad. Even if you *are* special, you don't have to—"

"Oh, no!" cried Annie. She covered her mouth with her hands.

"What?" said Jack, following her shocked gaze.

Jack's leather bag lay at Beauty's feet. It was open. Beside it was the torn leather cover of Aristotle's book. Wet pages hung in shreds from Beauty's mouth as she happily chewed the precious treasure.

CHAPTER EIGHT

Room of the Tree

"Nooooo!" cried Jack.

Jack ran to Beauty and yanked hunks of paper from her mouth. Annie dropped to her knees and picked up the torn pieces strewn around the camel's big feet.

"The treasure's ruined!" moaned Annie.

Jack was stunned. "I shouldn't have left my bag here," he said.

"No, it's all my fault. I shouldn't have gone back and bragged to those kids," wailed Annie.

"I should have acted more humble, like Merlin said." Annie sounded like she was about to cry.

"It's okay," said Jack. But he knew it wasn't. The book was destroyed. They'd failed in their mission.

"Maybe—maybe we can fix it," said Annie.

Jack shook his head. "No, we can't," he said. "It's completely destroyed. It can't be fixed."

Annie looked up. "What—what did you just say?" she said.

"I said it can't be fixed," said Jack.

A big grin crossed Annie's face. "Right! It can't be fixed!" she said. "Help me gather up all these pieces!"

"Why?" said Jack. Had Annie gone nuts?

"Just do it! Quick!" said Annie.

Jack and Annie rushed around the stable, gathering up all the torn pages.

"Now pile everything over here on top of the cover and give me the book," said Annie.

"What book?" said Jack.

"The rhyme book!" said Annie.

"Oh. Oh!" said Jack. "Right!" He reached into his shoulder bag and pulled out Teddy and Kathleen's book of magic rhymes.

Jack opened the book and read down the list. "Here it is: *Mend What Cannot Be Mended*," he said.

"That's the one," said Annie.

Jack flipped through the pages until he came to the rhyme. He held up the book so he and Annie could both see. Standing in a shaft of sunlight, Jack read in a loud, clear voice:

Heal what is broken beyond repair!

Annie read the second line:

Avi-bree-all! Fen-a-mare!

The paper bits fluttered. They began to swirl off the floor. They swirled up and around as if they were caught in a small tornado. The tornado captured all the torn pieces in its funnel and twisted them together. The papers swirled into a blur of blinding light.

Jack shielded his eyes. He heard a loud *whoof!* When he looked up, the bright tornado had vanished.

Lying on the floor of the stable in front of Jack and Annie was the ancient book.

Holding his breath, Jack carefully picked up the treasure. He opened the leather cover. "Oh, man," he whispered. Aristotle's priceless words of wisdom were neatly written on the yellow pages. There was no sign of a rip or tear anywhere.

"Thank goodness," breathed Annie.

"Yeah," said Jack.

"So what do we do now?" said Annie.

"I don't know," said Jack. "What's the next thing Merlin tells us to do?" He pulled out Merlin's letter and read:

Beneath birds who sing
in the Room of the Tree,
greet a friend you once knew
and a new friend to be.

"What's that mean?" said Jack.

Suddenly Jack heard someone behind them. He and Annie turned around. A girl was standing in the doorway of the stable. She wore a long white gown. Her hair and face were hidden by a veil.

"Hi," said Annie. "Who are you?"

"I am a servant of the palace," the girl whispered. "Come."

She motioned for them to follow her.

"Let's go," Annie said to Jack.

"Where is she taking us?" asked Jack. "And why is she whispering?"

"I don't know," said Annie. "But I feel like we should follow her."

"Okay," said Jack. He put the book of wisdom and the book of magic rhymes into his bag. He slung the bag over his shoulder and followed Annie and the servant girl out of the stable.

The three of them walked through the courtyard and through the palace doors. They walked down a wide candlelit hallway over a thick woven carpet.

At the end of the hallway was a tall, carved door. A boy servant stood by the door. He wore baggy trousers and a long shirt. His face was almost completely hidden by his head cloth. He did not speak or look at them.

The servant girl stood close to Jack and Annie. In her strange, whispery voice, she said, "In front of the chair, bow to the floor. Do not look up and do not speak until you are spoken to."

"But what—" said Jack.

"Go quickly," whispered the girl.

The boy servant pulled open the heavy door. The girl servant pushed them into the room.

"Wait," said Jack.

But the boy servant closed the door behind them, leaving Jack and Annie alone.

"Jack, look! We're here!" said Annie. "The Room of the Tree!"

Jack turned around. A giant tree stood in the

center of the room. It had silver leaves that fluttered as if blown by the wind. Mechanical golden birds sang *"Tweet-tweet!"* from the silver branches.

Beneath the strange tree was an empty black chair. Jewels sparkled in its shiny wood.

"We're in the right place," said Annie. She quoted from Merlin's letter:

Beneath birds who sing
in the Room of the Tree,
greet a friend you once knew
and a new friend to be.

"Another mystery solved," Annie said.

"Not really," said Jack. "Where are the two friends?"

"I don't know, but we better bow in front of the chair like that servant girl told us to," said Annie.

Jack and Annie knelt in front of the shiny black chair. They bowed their heads to the floor. Jack gripped his bag with the treasure inside.

"Remember what else she said," Annie reminded Jack. "Don't look up and don't speak until we're spoken to."

"But there's no one here," said Jack. He felt foolish, bowing in front of a chair and listening to the chirping of mechanical birds. *Why are we doing this?* he wondered.

The door opened with a low creaking sound. Jack squeezed his eyes shut. He heard footsteps moving past them.

"How did you get into the throne room?" a deep, gruff voice asked.

"A servant brought us here," said Annie.

"And why have you come?" asked the voice.

"We have a priceless treasure to give to the caliph of Baghdad," said Jack, keeping his head down. "It's a book of wisdom."

Jack fumbled in his bag and pulled out the book. He kept his eyes tightly shut as he held the book up toward the voice.

There was a long silence.

"We hope it will help the caliph spread wisdom to the world," said Annie.

"How did you come to be in possession of this book?" the man asked.

"We were helping a friend," said Annie. "And we got separated in a sandstorm."

"Ah, then I suppose you brought this book to Baghdad to gain a reward," said the man.

"No! No, we didn't," said Jack. "It was our mission to give it to the caliph."

"Surely you must be seeking some payment in exchange for this treasure," said the man. "Would you not like precious perfumes gathered from the sweetest flowers on earth?"

"No thank you," said Annie.

"Rubies as large as hens' eggs?" said the man.

"No thanks," said Jack.

"You would not accept the book's weight in gold?" said the man.

"We don't need a reward, really," said Jack.

"Since he likes books so much, why don't you

just tell the caliph to use his gold and rubies to buy more of them?" said Annie.

Again, there was silence. Then the man cleared his throat. When he spoke, his voice was gentle and familiar-sounding. "Look up at me, Jack and Annie," he said.

Jack opened his eyes. He slowly lifted his head. First he saw gleaming gold slippers . . . then a long white robe with gold trim . . . then a familiar face.

Jack gasped. He couldn't believe his eyes. The man wasn't a scary person at all. The man was Mamoon!

CHAPTER NINE

House of Wisdom

"Mamoon?" said Annie.

"Yes," said Mamoon. "I am very glad to see that you have safely arrived in Baghdad."

"We're glad you're safe, too!" said Annie. "We were worried about you."

"I looked everywhere for you after the sandstorm," said Mamoon. "Finally I gave up my search and returned sadly to Baghdad. I assume you found your family?"

"Uh, sure," said Annie, "we found them."

"And we found your book," said Jack. "When

we couldn't find you, we decided that we should give the book to the caliph."

Mamoon smiled. "You still do not understand, do you?" he said.

"Understand what?" said Annie.

"I am Caliph Abdullah al-Mamoon."

"*You're* the caliph?" said Annie.

"But—how—what?" stammered Jack.

"For many years, I have wanted a book of Aristotle's wisdom," explained the caliph. "I heard that such a book had been found in the city of Damascus, and I made arrangements to acquire it for my library. It was most important that it arrive here safely. I have long wished to travel again through the desert as I did when I was a boy. So I disguised myself as a humble merchant and made the journey. My fellow travelers never knew my true identity."

"Wow," whispered Jack.

"You have shown me that you have a great respect for books and learning," said Caliph al-Mamoon. "And you have also proven you have humble hearts. Before you join your family, I want to show you a very special place. I call it the House of Wisdom."

"*The House of Wisdom?*" breathed Jack. "That sounds great."

"It is my hope that the world will indeed find it 'great,'" said the caliph. "Come." He started to leave the room. Jack and Annie rose from the floor and hurried after him.

Carrying the ancient book of Aristotle, the caliph led Jack and Annie out of the Room of the Tree. His gold-trimmed robe billowed about him as he swept down the corridor. Every person he passed bowed low to the floor.

"Another mystery solved!" Annie said to Jack. She quoted from Merlin's letter:

Greet a friend you once knew
and a new friend to be.

"Both friends are the same person!" said Annie. "Mamoon from the desert and Caliph Abdullah al-Mamoon."

"Right," said Jack, smiling.

The caliph led Jack and Annie out the front doors of the palace. In the courtyard stood two camels with long poles attached to their saddles. Resting on top of the poles was a small carriage decorated with gold tassels and brass bells.

Servants helped Jack, Annie, and Caliph Abdullah al-Mamoon into the strange little carriage. Bells jingled as the camels began to move slowly through the courtyard.

The caliph opened tiny shutters to let in air and sunlight. Jack looked out. Everyone bowed as the royal carriage passed by: the boys playing ball, the gardeners weeding flower beds, the women carrying pots.

Jack had lots of questions about the House of Wisdom. But now that he knew their friend Mamoon was the mighty caliph, he felt shy. Even Annie seemed to be at a loss for words as they rode past the date palms and the palace gardens.

"We are here," said the caliph as the camels came to a stop. He helped Jack and Annie out of the carriage. Then he led them up the steps of a large brick building.

"Welcome to the House of Wisdom," said the caliph, "a learning center for the entire world."

"What happens here?" asked Jack.

"Come, I will show you." The caliph escorted Jack and Annie through the front door and down a wide hallway. "We have a laboratory for discovering new medicines," he said, "and an observatory for viewing the stars and planets. But *this* is my favorite room of all."

The caliph stopped before an arched doorway. He opened the door and led Jack and Annie into a huge, silent room. "This is the library," he said in a hushed voice. "Even I must be very quiet here."

Late-afternoon light slanted down from high, open windows, streaming over bookshelves and colorful carpets. Men read at long tables. When the readers looked up and saw the caliph, they all started to rise.

"Please continue with your work. Do not mind us," the caliph said softly.

The men sat down again and returned to their reading and writing.

The caliph pointed to a bearded man sitting by a window, hunched over a pile of papers. The man was writing furiously.

"That is al-Khwarizmi," whispered the caliph. "He is a truly great mathematician. He has perfected the Indian way of writing numbers." The caliph pointed to numbers written on a board on the wall: *1, 2, 3, 4, 5, 6, 7, 8, 9, 10*. "We call these the Arabic numerals," he said.

"Arabic numerals?" said Jack.

"Yes," said the caliph.

Jack whispered to Annie, "We use the Arabic numerals, too. They must have come from that guy."

The caliph pointed to another man reading by the window. "He is al-Kindi. He is perhaps the most brilliant scientist and thinker in the world," whispered the caliph. "But he is very humble. He believes knowledge cannot belong to only one person or country. It belongs to all. The world grows wise only when wisdom is shared. I agree. And that is why I built this house."

"I agree, too," whispered Annie.

"Me too," said Jack.

"Scientists and scholars from many countries come here to read and study and share their knowledge," whispered the caliph. "We have thousands of books. They have all been copied by hand."

"By *hand*?" said Annie. "That's a *lot* of writing!"

"What kind of books?" asked Jack.

"Books of history, mathematics, geography, and medicine," said the caliph. "But we also have a very special book of fantasy and wonder."

The caliph took a large, thick book down from a shelf. He rested it on a table and turned the pages to show Jack and Annie. The book was filled with fancy writing and beautiful illustrations. There were pictures of Aladdin and Ali Baba, magic lamps and flying carpets.

"Oh, *Tales from the Arabian Nights*!" said Annie. "We know those stories."

"You do? Wonderful!" the caliph said with a smile. "It seems someone from our land has traveled to yours and shared our stories. Perhaps someone will soon bring stories from your land back to us. That is the great power of a book, no?"

"Yes," said Annie.

"And I hope your land will hear of this book, too, someday," said the caliph. He held up the book of Aristotle's writings. "After I have read it, I will have it copied so I can share its wisdom with the world. Thank you for helping me."

"Sure," Jack said modestly. "That was our mission."

"I fear I must now return to my duties," said the caliph. "But please, stay in the library. Read until you must go to meet your family. And come back someday to visit me."

"We'll try," said Jack.

"Good-bye, Annie. Good-bye, Jack."

"Bye, Mamoon," Annie said.

The mighty caliph gave them a warm smile and a deep bow. Then he left Jack and Annie in his wondrous library.

CHAPTER TEN

Before the Moon Rises

Jack and Annie looked around the big room. The scholars and scientists were all deep into their reading.

"I can't believe Mamoon is the caliph," whispered Jack.

"*Remember that life is full of surprises,*" Annie repeated from Merlin's letter.

"Yeah, and *Return to the tree house before the moon rises,*" Jack finished.

"I almost forgot that part," said Annie.

"Me too," said Jack.

"Shh!" said one of the scholars and scientists.

"Sorry," said Annie.

Jack and Annie looked up at the open window. The sky was pink. The sun would be setting soon. "We have to get back to the tree house," Annie whispered, "before the moon rises."

"I know," said Jack, "but how?" He felt a moment of panic. *The tree house is really far away*, he thought. *If we traveled on Beauty and Cutie, it would take a whole day and night to get there. And what about sandstorms? And bandits?* Jack looked at Annie.

She was smiling. *Magic*, she mouthed.

Jack caught his breath and nodded. They both looked around to see if any of the scholars or scientists were watching. They weren't.

Jack quietly slipped Teddy and Kathleen's book out of his bag. He and Annie turned their backs to the others and opened the book to the table of contents.

Annie pointed to *Turn into Ducks*.

Jack gave her a look.

Annie pointed to *Fly Through the Air*.

"Yes!" said Jack.

"Shh!" said a scholar.

Jack turned to the right page. He held up the book so they both could see.

Jack said the first line of the rhyme:

Sail through the sky where you wish to go!

Annie said the second:

Sawn-ee-fore, sawn-ee-row!

"You must be quiet, or you will have to leave the library!" one of the scholars said grouchily.

"Don't worry, we're going," said Annie.

A wind blew through the tall open window, fluttering the pages of the *Arabian Nights* book. The scholars and scientists grabbed their papers before they blew away.

The wind picked up a corner of the small carpet Jack and Annie were standing on. The carpet rippled. Jack and Annie fell forward. As they tried to stand, the carpet lifted off the floor.

"Oh!" cried all the scholars and scientists.

The carpet began floating up. It rose above

the long tables. It rose above the shelves of books. Everyone jumped out of their chairs and scrambled out of the way, shouting, "Help!"—"Move!"—"Watch out!"—"Impossible!"—"What is happening?"

"Bye!" called Annie.

The carpet floated to the tall open window and glided out of the House of Wisdom.

Chilly air blew against Jack and Annie. Their head cloths flapped wildly as they clung to the end of the carpet and sailed through the sky.

"This is great!" cried Jack.

"*Really* great!" shouted Annie.

The carpet soared over the House of Wisdom, over the caliph riding back to his palace in his carriage, and over the camel stable.

The carpet zipped over the green dome with the horse on top. It flew over the courtyard, where the boys were still playing ball, over the third wall, and past the green field and the grand avenue.

The carpet flew over the second wall, the houses, the hospitals, and the hundred lions in the zoo. It flew over the first wall, the arched bridge, and the moat.

The carpet zoomed over the bazaar with the maze of stalls, the shoemakers, potters, and weavers. It sailed high over the road to Baghdad. Below, Jack and Annie saw the men driving donkey carts, the boys leading sheep, and the women carrying pots.

The carpet flew faster and faster and faster—
over the river, the grazing fields,
and the dunes with the whistling sands,
over the red glowing desert
toward the setting sun
and the small oasis
in the middle of nowhere.

The magic carpet slid smoothly onto the scrubby grass, near the small spring and the thorny shrubs, near the date palms and the rope ladder.

The desert looked as if it were on fire with golden red light. Jack felt giddy. "That—that was so fast!" he said. "I can't believe we made it all the way here."

"No kidding," said Annie. "The magic must have helped us stay on."

She and Jack tried to stand. They teetered and fell against each other.

"Steady," said Annie, giggling. "You okay?"

"Perfect," said Jack. He put his bag over his shoulder and staggered off the carpet. Then he and Annie headed over to the tallest date palm. Jack pulled the rope ladder from behind the trunk, and they climbed up.

When they got inside the tree house, Jack took out Merlin's letter. He glanced out the window one last time.

The sun was gone. The carpet looked small and ordinary in the shadows beneath the palm tree. The desert looked vast and silent and lonely. A thin crescent moon had appeared in the sky.

"*Return to the tree house before the moon rises*," said Jack.

"That was our last instruction from Merlin," said Annie. "We're all done."

Jack looked down at Merlin's letter. He pointed at the words *Jack and Annie of Frog Creek*. "I wish we could go home!" he said.

The wind started to blow.

The tree house started to spin.

It spun faster and faster.

Then everything was still.

Absolutely still.

🐫 🐫 🐫

The Frog Creek woods were chilly in the afternoon air. Jack and Annie were dressed in their jeans and jackets again. Jack's shoulder bag was a backpack.

"Good trip," Jack said simply.

Annie nodded. "Really cool," she said.

"I guess we should get home," said Jack. "I have lots of homework to finish."

"Leave the research book. But don't forget to

take Teddy and Kathleen's rhyme book for safe-keeping," said Annie.

Jack reached into his backpack. He pulled out the book on the golden age of Baghdad and placed it on the tree house floor. Then he threw his pack over his shoulder and climbed down the ladder. Annie followed. Together they walked through the early-spring woods.

"We passed Merlin's second test," said Annie. "We helped spread wisdom to the world. . . . That's a pretty big deal."

"Be humble," Jack reminded her.

"Well, I guess Teddy and Kathleen's book did the hard stuff for us," Annie said humbly.

"I miss them," said Jack.

"Me too," said Annie. "But I think they might have been with us in Baghdad."

"What do you mean?" said Jack.

"Remember that servant girl and boy who took us to the caliph?" said Annie. "They sort of came out of nowhere. And we never actually saw their faces, did we?"

"No . . . ," said Jack. "You think?"

Annie shrugged. "Maybe."

Jack smiled and took a deep breath. "Maybe," he said softly.

"Two missions and five rhymes left," said Annie. "I hope Merlin sends for us again soon."

"But not *too* soon," said Jack. "I need to do my homework first."

Annie laughed. "Math with Arabic numerals?" she said.

"Right," said Jack. "And maybe tomorrow we'll go to the library and see if they have any books of Aristotle's wisdom."

"Good idea," said Annie.

A cool spring breeze rustled the trees, and Jack and Annie hurried toward home.

More Facts About Baghdad

Baghdad is an ancient city that lies between the Tigris and Euphrates rivers. Long ago, this area was called Mesopotamia, which means "between the rivers." Today this land is called Iraq, and Baghdad is its capital.

The character of Mamoon in this book was inspired by *two* caliphs of Baghdad in the ninth century—Harun al-Rashid and his son Abdullah al-Mamoon (often spelled al-Mamoun).

It is said that Harun al-Rashid sometimes disguised himself and went to the bazaars to listen to his people. The world of al-Rashid was the inspiration for the collection of stories known as *A Thousand and One Nights* or *Tales from the Arabian Nights*.

Abdullah al-Mamoon was the youngest son of Harun al-Rashid. He carried on his father's work by honoring the arts and sciences. He also founded the House of Wisdom in Baghdad.

The House of Wisdom was a home to scholars from all over the Eastern world. Two important thinkers who studied there were al-Kindi, who was called "the philosopher of the Arabs," and the mathematician al-Khwarizmi, who introduced algebra (a kind of math) to the world.

Many ancient writings were stored and translated at the House of Wisdom. Some of the most important writings included the work of the Greek philosopher Aristotle. Aristotle's teachings helped lay the foundation for modern science.

Harun al-Rashid helped start a golden age, in which Baghdad would be an important center of learning and culture for the next four hundred years. In 1258, the city was destroyed by Mongol invaders.

Fun Activities for Jack and Annie and *You*!

Puzzle of the Sandstorms

Jack and Annie learned many new things on their adventure in ancient Baghdad. Did you? Put your knowledge to the test with this puzzle. You can use a notebook or make a copy of this page if you don't want to write in your book.

From 762 AD to 1258 AD, the Arab world had a _____ age.

◯ ☐ ☐ ☐ ☐ ☐

A ruler known as a _____ governed the Arab empire.

☐ ☐ ☐ ☐ ☐ ◯

A windstorm that can cause travelers to lose their way in the desert.

☐ ◯ ☐ ☐ ☐ ☐ ☐ ☐ ☐ ☐

The fruit of the desert, it grows on a kind of palm tree.

◯ ☐ ☐ ☐

An animal known as the "ship of the desert."

☐ ◯ ☐ ☐ ☐

A huge open-air market where items were traded, bought, and sold.

◯ ☐ ☐ ☐ ☐ ☐

A library and a home to scholars in the ancient world: the House of _____.

☐ ☐ ☐ ◯ ☐ ☐

Now look at your answers above. The letters that are circled spell a word—but that word is scrambled! Can you unscramble the letters to spell the name of an ancient city?

Desert Dessert

Jack and Annie discovered that dates were an important food in the Middle East during the Golden Age of Baghdad.

Today, dates are grown in many places. Most of the dates in the United States are grown in California. That means you don't have to travel to the desert and shake a date palm to get your hands on the "fruit of the desert." You can find it at most grocery stores!

Dates are good for you and can be eaten on their own or as part of a recipe. Ask an adult to help you try the recipe below.

Date & Chocolate Chip Cookies

2¼ cups all-purpose flour

1 teaspoon baking soda

1 teaspoon salt

1 cup butter, softened

¾ cup sugar

¾ cup brown sugar

2 large eggs, beaten

1 teaspoon vanilla

2 cups semisweet chocolate chips

1 cup dried dates, chopped

1. Preheat oven to 375°F.

2. In a bowl, combine flour, baking soda, and salt. Set aside until step 5.

3. In a second, larger bowl, mash the butter, sugar, and brown sugar together until the butter has soaked up the sugar.

4. Mix the eggs and vanilla into the butter/sugar until the mixture is smooth.

5. Little by little, add the flour mixture to the butter mixture until everything is mixed together. The batter should be gooey.

6. Stir in chips and dates.

7. Drop round teaspoonfuls of batter onto ungreased cookie sheets. (The cookies will flatten and spread out as they bake.) You should have enough for about 80 cookies.

8. Bake 8 to 10 minutes or until golden brown. Let them cool, and then enjoy!

Sand Science

Here's a simple experiment that you can do with sand from the beach or a hardware store.

1. Fill a drinking glass with sand.

Do you think there is anything in the glass with the sand? Why or why not?

2. Slowly pour some water on top of the sand.

What happens?

There is room for the water to fit in the glass. That's because when you fill a container with sand, there is still *air* between the small grains of sand.

The water took the place of the air. Did you see bubbles? If you did, that's the air being moved out of the way by the water.

So even when you say a glass is "full" of sand, there is still room for air . . . or water!

The Ancient Art of Papermaking

Paper was invented in China more than two thousand years ago. But it took a long time for paper to spread to other parts of the world. In the eighth century, the secrets of papermaking came to the Arab world.

Before paper, people would write on *papyrus* or *parchment*. Papyrus was woven from plants. Parchment was made of animal skin. Both were rare and expensive.

But paper could be made from rags or trees. It was not expensive. It was not difficult to make. That meant more books could be made. It meant more people could write down information. Paper made reading and writing important for everyone, not just rich people.

Here is a recipe for making your own paper. While paper is now made in factories known as *paper mills*, you can still make it by hand the way Mamoon's people would have done long ago.

You will need:
window screen
construction paper or paper tissues
blender (or electric mixer and bowl)
starch
shallow pan
newspapers
rolling pin
an adult to help you

1. Start with a piece of window screen, which you can get at a hardware or craft store. Cut it to the size you want your piece of paper to be, then bend the edges over so that the screen has a "frame." (You can also use duct tape to cover any sharp edges.)

2. Tear up enough tissue or construction paper to make ⅛ cup of firmly packed scraps.

3. Put the scraps in a blender. Then fill the blender with hot water until it is about two-thirds full.

4. Blend for about 45 seconds, or until your pulp is a "slurry." Add a tablespoon of starch.

5. Pour the slurry into a shallow pan. A 9" x 12" casserole dish works well.

6. Slide the screen to the bottom of the inside of the pan. Gently move it around so that the slurry spreads out over the screen.

7. Lift the screen straight up and out of the pan. The screen should be covered with a layer of pulp. Hold the screen in the air for a minute to allow some of the water to drip back into the pan.

8. Place the screen (and its pulp) on top of a stack of newspaper.

9. Put more newspaper on top. Roll a rolling pin over the newspaper stack to squeeze out extra water.

10. Lift off the top newspapers to uncover the screen. Gently peel the homemade paper from the screen.

11. Place the homemade paper on another, dry stack of newspaper and allow it to dry completely (this may take several days). You can reuse the screen as often as you want!

Use Your Research Skills

When Jack used his research book to learn about dates, he was interrupted before he could finish.

> **Not only are dates an important food, but the wood and leaves of the date palm are used to make—**

Jack didn't have time to read the rest. Can you finish the sentence?

What can you make using the wood and leaves of a tree like the date palm?

First make a guess.

Then use your research skills to find an answer. (Hint: There is more than one correct answer.)

What did you find? Was your first guess correct?

Here's a special preview of

Magic Tree House®
MERLIN MISSIONS #7
NIGHT OF THE NEW MAGICIANS

Jack and Annie go on another amazing
adventure filled with history, magic . . .
and amazing inventions!

Available now!

Excerpt copyright © 2006 by Mary Pope Osborne.
Illustrations copyright © 2006 by Sal Murdocca. Published by Random House
Children's Books, a division of Penguin Random House LLC, New York.

CHAPTER ONE

Four New Magicians

Jack sat on the porch, reading in the summer twilight. Crickets chirped in the Frog Creek woods. The bell of an ice cream truck jingled down the street.

Annie stepped out the front door. "Let's go," she said.

"Where?" said Jack.

"Mom gave us money for ice cream," said Annie.

"Cool," said Jack. He pulled on his backpack. Then he followed Annie down the porch steps.

As they headed up the sidewalk, the smell of damp leaves and moss wafted from the woods.

Annie stopped walking. "Listen," she said.

Jack listened. "What?" he said. "I don't hear anything."

"That's the *point*," said Annie. "A minute ago, the crickets were blaring away. Now everything's super quiet."

Jack listened again. Annie was right. All the Frog Creek woods seemed to be holding its breath.

"Do you think . . . ?" said Jack.

"Maybe," said Annie, grinning. "Let's go check!"

Jack and Annie hurried across the street and into the dimly lit woods. They walked quickly between the leafy trees, until they came to the tallest oak. A rope ladder dangled from the treetop. The magic tree house sat high in the branches, catching the last light of day.

Jack smiled. "I guess ice cream will have to wait," he said.

"Yep," said Annie. She grabbed the ladder and climbed up. Jack climbed up after her.

Inside the tree house, dusky light filtered through the window. Lying on the wooden floor was a folded piece of paper and a slim book with a red cover.

Annie grabbed the paper. Jack picked up the book. "This must be a research book from Morgan," he said.

The book's title was written in gold letters:

Guide Book:
Paris World's Fair
~1889~

"Paris World's Fair?" said Jack.

"That sounds like fun!" said Annie.

"Yeah, but I wonder why we're going there," said Jack.

"This should tell us," said Annie. She unfolded the paper. "It's Merlin's handwriting." She read aloud:

To Jack and Annie of Frog Creek:
I have discovered that an evil sorcerer is plotting to steal the secrets of four new magicians at the Paris World's Fair.

Your mission is to find the magicians, warn them, and learn their secrets for me. The four new magicians are:

The Magician of Sound—
his voice can be heard
for a thousand miles.

The Magician of Light—
his fires glow,
but they do not burn.

The Magician of the Invisible—
he battles deadly enemies
no one can see.

The Magician of Iron—
he bends the metals of earth
and triumphs over the wind.

Good luck,
M.

"Our mission sounds more like a fairy tale than real life," said Jack. "An evil sorcerer. Magicians of the Invisible, Light, Sound, and Iron. They sound like they belong in a magical place like Camelot, not a real place like Paris, France."

"But we're going to a World's Fair," said Annie. "That sounds kind of magical, doesn't it?"

"Maybe," said Jack. "But why do such powerful magicians need our help in the first place? Why can't they defeat the evil sorcerer with their own powers?"

"Maybe the sorcerer's power is stronger than theirs," said Annie.

"So maybe we can help them with Teddy and Kathleen's rhymes," said Jack.

Annie gasped. "Oh, no! We need the rhyme book! We have to go back home and get it!"

"Don't worry, I have it," said Jack. "Ever since we got back from Baghdad, I've been taking it with me everywhere I go—just in case Merlin sends for us."

"Whew," said Annie. "Let's take a look."

Jack reached into his backpack. He pulled out the small book written by their two young sorcerer friends from Camelot:

10 MAGIC RHYMES FOR ANNIE AND JACK FROM TEDDY AND KATHLEEN

Jack turned to the table of contents. "Okay, we've used five rhymes on our last two missions," he said. "So we have five left for the next two. We haven't used *Spin into the Air*, or *Make Something Disappear*, or *Pull a Cloud from the Sky,* or *Find a Treasure You Must Never Lose,* or *Turn into Ducks.*"

"Quack! Quack!"

Jack looked up.

"Just kidding," said Annie.

"You'd better not make jokes about these rhymes," Jack said. "You might end up saying the wrong one at the wrong time and really get us in trouble." He closed the rhyme book. "Ready to go?"

"Ready," said Annie.

Jack took a deep breath and picked up the guide book to the 1889 Paris World's Fair. He pointed to the title. "I wish we could go there," he said.

The wind started to blow.

The tree house started to spin.

It spun faster and faster.

Then everything was still.

Absolutely still.

Track the facts with Jack and Annie!

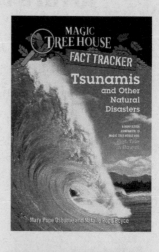

Magic Tree House® Fact Trackers are the must-have,
all-true companions to your favorite
Magic Tree House® adventures!

Enough cool facts
to fill a tree house!

Jack and Annie have been all over the world in their adventures in the magic tree house. And they've learned lots of incredible facts along the way. Now they want to share them with you! Get ready for a collection of the weirdest, grossest, funniest, most all-around amazing facts that Jack and Annie have ever encountered. It's the ultimate fact attack!

Magic Tree House®

Magic Tree House® Merlin Missions

Magic Tree House® Super Edition

#1: World at War, 1944

Magic Tree House® Fact Trackers

More Magic Tree House®